First published in Great Britain in
MA Publishing course at the Univ

This book is a work of fiction. Names, characters,
businesses, organisations, places, and events are
either the product of the author's imagination or are
used fictitiously. Any resemblance to actual persons,
living or dead, events or locales is completely
coincidental.

The cover has been designed and created by Emily
Birch.

www.emilybirch.co.uk

This ebook has been collected, typeset, and edited by
Paige Briscoe.

www.wordsfromthepaige.wordpress.com

# Devil's Lettuce

# About the Author

Mary-Jane does not exist. She is a collective pseudonym for all of the participants in this book so that their individual identities could be protected, as currently under UK law marijuana is a class B substance that is not legal for personal use.

Each submission has been included with explicit permission from the original authors, and no identifiable information has been included. If you have contributed to the works of Mary-Jane, you have my utmost gratitude for making this project possible.

This book has not encouraged the breaking of UK law, and any participant has done so voluntarily and at their own risk.

# About This Book

This anthology is comprised of short stories, poems, and streams of consciousness writings, that have been constructed whilst their respective authors were under the influence of THC. Tetrahydrocannabinol (THC) is the psychoactive ingredient found in the Cannabis plant, a part of Cannabacceae family that are also known as Hemp plants. This is what creates the effect of feeling high when smoked, or otherwise consumed.

Submissions within this collection remain largely unedited in order to preserve the integrity of the piece, and further exhibit the intent of this publication: to showcase the creative workings of the mind whilst, pardon the pun, one is out of their mind. Only spelling corrections and minor grammatical improvements have been made, and only in places where required to in order to aid in the coherency of a piece. Therefore, you may spot many irregularities that deviate from standard English.

Happy reading, and happy smoking.

# Contents

## Two Little Ducks

Two little duckies floating downstream,

Towards the embankment, green

But the mud gurgles, and the water boils,

And the eye blinks open, to end the dream

Two little duckies begin to scream

(quack)

      (quack)

            (quack)

                  (quack)

## Beelzebub's Broccoli

It grows by the riverbank

The Nightmare Dank

One wee puff of Screaming Green,

Five visions of hell + perhaps of veg seen

The florets of fire, the stems of Hell

Blaze it baby

I will as well.

## Broken

I once read that broken jugs and mugs
can be fixed by pure gold

Stitched back whole.

When

I lose myself to my fragments,

When I shatter

And I can't keep myself whole

If you then tried to stitch me with gold

I'd ask you to cradle my reincarnation in
your hands,

Hold these fragments like a china mug of
tea,

Let the warmth of me soak into your
skin,

Lift what remains of me to your lips,

Drink me until I empty and you have
savoured every part of me,

And when you are left with the bitter bite
of me,

An aftertaste too much to bear,

Let me fall apart in your hands,

Drift slowly and softly through your fingers,

Until I'm no longer salvageable.

## Sunday

The black sludge streaked the back of her calves as she trudged for the train home.

Home.

Co-inhabited with the kindly stranger,

Friend?

Thoughts swirling the space in her head like the wind to her hair.

Security shattered. Alone. A fool.

The shame reflected in the empty window of the station. A smile.

Filling the emptiness with the touch of a stranger; a fool.

Trembling hands search blindly in pockets for a lighter. Adrenaline, oxytocin coursing her veins.

Add nicotine.

The affair. The tsunami that sows the seed.

His affair.

Call it off, continue, dilemma;

Pathetic.

The harsh lights of the carriage distort
the passing world,

Warp speed. The cacophony of silence.

Her mind,

A blur.

Headphones. The Clash to drown out the
noise. Plugged in to tranquillity.

Crowds move in the cyclic snail pace
rush for home.

## Irrational

Hands against the sweat
the cold the feel of my hands 209
degrees hotter than anything wait-
type error 100 degrees meant-
hiccups.
Fuck me is that Marcy?
A silhouette, identical.

## Seasons

Throughout the seasons of growth, strength, bloom and death.

What do we take for granted?

Is it the beauty of conception? Or the life it shares from its own core?

Maybe the distraction from the impending season change of your own.

We ache for the longing to understand when our season is nigh.

The itch of lack of understanding, the aching to find our own vitality.

When my season has arrived, I hope I will know.

## Repeat

I was sitting here just thinking,

How sad a life must be,

To have nothing more to do in a day than smoke a bit of weed.

The daily conversation consists of - 'you got rizzla?' 'you got piece?'

But I guess none of that really matters when you finally sit there lean.

See don't think I misunderstand the feeling when it finally sets you free,

It's just that I remember it wearing off and being faced with reality.

So when you're lying in your bed after a late night sesh,

And you think to yourself 'what's happened to my head?'

Then you realise that you have smoked it all away,

Because it's the only way that you know how to deal with the pain-

But you're going insane, the feelings staying the same, the rising pressure pulsates around your body and brain,

You look out of the window but you only
see rain

So the only choice you have is to go and
do it again.

# Winter White

Forever pour spirit in my bars

Unlike vice and co

Grab a mic and I'll slice your throat

Pass the knife and I'll focus on mine for jokes

It turned out my life's awoken

Passed away

Is the nicest bloke

With violent strokes

Prescribed the dope

It didn't work so he tried the rope

It wasn't tight enough

Then the Titan enlightened us

With the white dust

For your plants to feed on

Everything eats isn't free from

Please stop watching the way that I squirm

When the earth's grave wagers a worm

I waive any claims that my fragrance is firm

But it's strange that today

My dear saviour emerged

And I watched as they burned

Bare flames for the purge of the virgin

Work didn't work to deter him

Skirmish of vermin

Fertile and gurning

Detergent is urgent for certain

Deep within simple minds

Winter white

Mysticism intertwined

If you think I'm listening

You clearly missed a trick in life

Sinful vibe

Must avoid pizza

Man, someone give the kid a slice

Stop '@'-ing me

It's not an allergy

I may rap deep but no one clocks my analogies

That's just 'cause they're shit

Iridescent spit drips

Descending from his effervescent lips

From the terror-ridden bliss

When he'd evidently trip

From the pengest of his spliffs

And a belly full of Sid

An absolutely fine mix of Hennessy, Elyx

Disturbing concentration like Dachau

Bell up Ben Mitchell to get you slapped down

Always mad proud of his crap town

Sad clown with a shattered frown

Snatch the crown

Bell up Poseidon

Begging for his trident

Never sell my psilocybin

Cloning castor like its natural

He necks the ricin

Dad's working hard to be factual

I bet he's lying

Now my minds split from the lysin

And twice as creepy

Like the twins from the shining.

## Celery and a Smoothie

Why do I keep forgetting to bring a
backup lighter out with me?

Healthiest stoned snack ever, celery and
a smoothie.

If you wanna know what it's like to be
me right now, just

listen to 1975's 'Frail State of Mind'

a few times a day for like three weeks.

Celery and a smoothie. That's me.

I'm worried, my rabbits are turning their
nose up

at a bit of celery, I ate so much.

What is wrong with the celery?!

I miss Boy cuddles.

'Novocaine' by Frank Ocean SLAPS whilst
high.

Felt it through my bod.

I really like using sus for suspicious, I
like the way it sounds.

## Heartstrings

Sharp strings of the violin,

Tug tug tugging-

Heartstrings, heartstrings-

But the soft, thick, so soft

(Like silk like cotton candy off a cloud)

Pluck pluck plucking,

Playing notes of you, notes of me.

## The Rich Lady

The fur bobbing with the current could have been a fox's tail, tangled with a fallen branch; but it wasn't. She knew it was fake fur from a coat. The drowned body it had been attached to had long floated away but it, dancing with the river, holding the branch, remained. The sound of water filled the space she might have called for help in. Instead, she watched on.

## The Wooden Lady

Two legs in the air; it could almost be a vertically impaled body. A tree sprouts through the branches of her legs, her ostrich head hidden amongst the roots and the leaves. Thin veins like branches reaching up to the heavens- damned to be twigs. A wooden lady sacrificed to the earth spirits, once home to lost boys and glitter, now glimmering in the reflection of the river (off whose bank she resides). She's home to the birds and the squirrel and the rustling leaves now.

## The Flying Lady

If you spot a leaf or a blossom falling at
the edge of summer, be sure to find its
reflection in the river. Stare as hard as
you can as it flies through the current of
life, from the current of the air to the
current of the water, if you're lucky
enough to witness the moment of
impact, in the outstretching ripples you'll
see a thing of beauty. The jagged and
ever-changing reflection of the spine of
the world. A falling leaf makes ripples in
the current of your life, the light
bouncing off the waves will show you.

## Half and Half

The Top Halves watches their Bottom Halves splash along the stones, the chilly water drowning their toes.

"Some curse this is, eh?" said a Top Half, their torso resting on a bench, hands gripping tight.

The Bottom Halves needed to be watered in running water - if they dried up, the Top Half would start to dry, crack, burn. The Top Half needed to watch- if they looked away, the Bottom Halves would fall, confused and lost, float downstream.

"To be a whole person, innit," said a Top Half.

One day, a Bottom might stride off on their own without being seen, and slip away. A Top might turn away to gaze at the sky, and be ok. One day.

## And All because I took a toke.

There stood a mid-summer dawn, with a light breeze an opening so mystical the forest enticed those willing like a siren to the sea unbeknownst to the perfect storm. How would someone handle this without the keen need for cannabis? A crackle slices the atmospheric fog and becomes inhaled through the first take. A chirp of birds, the rustling of leaves, a feeling of ease flows. Depression cracks a smile for the special occasion as the paths light for no other; a sinful strut begins as he travels down a path he knows for only consisting of gravel.

A second puff to elongate the dark narrow brambles. A strive for something to ease those thoughts that weren't his with each passing moment lasting an eternity in his mind. Something was different. A once alluring pallet of green had become a monochromatic blur of murky whispers. Happiness fades with the sun - if this was even still a reality.

An anxious fleshy train now trudged down a once familiar path with primal fear to where he once was lost cannot describe. A line of reality gone with another drag; he keeps smoking as that's all he knows now. Nothing could have prepared him for such a walk.

Hours go by, stuck in this refer madness, every view is familiar but yet detached from memory. Days turn to months to years without any sight of the sun.

He doesn't know who he is, what he is, or why he's here. What was once infinite potential erodes into a concoction of undiagnosable disorders. An opening of light shines through exposing the woeful pallet once again. He exists knowing he can't look back in fear that the voices aren't whole. He doesn't know if he will ever remember what he is. Maybe one day he'll return, forgetting the path he took that lead him there.

## Snippets of a Different Life

"FUCK."

Standing on the singular, seagull shit splattered platform of Aberystwyth train station the lone word cuts through the dark expanse of my skull. The foghorn sound to the lighthouse that is my brain. A flash of warning light: FUCK... darkness. A flash; FUCK... darkness.

The weekends' conversations rise to the surface of my brain, reminding me once again of the shame I should probably feel, but don't.

*

"Eurgh. Jesus wept, where am I?"

"Allroyt, It's only Jayums."

Oh how the dulcet tones of your ex boyfriends' Birmingham accent cut like a rusted chainsaw through a comedown.

"How ya feelen space cadet, want a smoke?"

God I resent him sometimes. Of course I want to smoke, I'm dying. "Green?"

"Always fer ma star gazer."

The passive aggressive pet names are out in full force this morning. All the signs of an upset James. I wonder what I did this time?

Turning his back to me to hide the flushed cheeks he started to skin up.

"ow was lus noight then?"

I couldn't help but smile. This was something I found incredibly endearing about him. Five years together had taught me his attempts to start a 'serious' conversation.

Our relationship ended over six months ago. James wanted to pursue his career overseas following a promotion; envisioning me there with him. I wasn't prepared for the commitment, so politely declined the offer of America along with, it turned out, the future of our relationship.

Weeks of agonising over how and if long distance would work culminated in the decision to part ways.

"Yeh was good. Sarah did the most ridiculous thing."

"I'm not surprised."

Silence. He sparks up looking away from me to the window. Sitting cross legged on the bean stool we stole from a shisha bar in Soho two years prior, he reminds me of the shy, nerdy 22-year-old hidden in a bulk of muscle and tattoo I first met.

He catches and holds my eye, smiling. As he takes a drag he stands and walks towards me. Crouching beside the bed he drapes his arm over my shoulder and puts the joint between my lips.

I suck at the roach like an asthmatic in attack. Sweet nectar. Yes.

"So, I've been thinking about America."

Ex-fucking-scuse me? Interest… piqued. I keep his eye contact but don't say anything.

"Yeh, so just... America. I err, spoke to my company..."

OH SWEET JESUS. He hasn't done what I think...

I need his arm off me.

I shuffle from laying on my side to sitting; my back against the wall with knees tucked to my chest, arm wrapped around my shins, chin resting on one knee. I look over his head to the space beyond this conversation.

"...I've decided to take a lower position in London instead."

Yeh. He did what I thought. Oh lord.

"That way it won't be so difficult for us long-distance wise, and maybe we can make things work us both?"

So this is how you tell your ex that since your breakup six months ago you've scouted the singles market every weekend with the vigour of what is only comparable to that of a rabbit in heat? Ah, interesting. I thought I would NEVER have to tell him.

The plan was to gracefully disappear into the Scottish countryside. You know, real quiet-like.

Never to return. Okay, that's excessive. But I didn't plan to see him so soon. I had hoped it would be in years' time, he would have found a new perfect American girlfriend, I'd be doing... something and oh how we would all laugh at how well everything turned out: like a cheesy rom-com. Ideal.

I did not envision the events of this weekend.

*

James is everything I wanted.

Glasgow is everything I want.

Shit.

Following the breakup, I upped sticks and moved to Scotland. Living in our tiny welsh town without James proved difficult. A long time had passed since James. Six months with no contact until a mutual friend, Sarah's birthday. A weekend with pals in a chalet on the coast… perfect. If he weren't there.

I was single. I was dating… or a looser form of the kind.

And James throws that at me.

When I'm THIS hungover?

\*

I remember our first date.

"You never said you were from Birmingham?"

"Ha, yeh, didn't think ter mention it loike. Nelly everyone at yooni eya is a Brummy. Is it an issue fer yaouw?"

It absolutely was an issue. There is no possible way he can whisper 'good girl' into my ear with that accent and expect me to take him seriously.

But I didn't say that. I was far too aware of the size of his hands and the tattoos covering his body - visible through his extremely tight, fresh salmon pink shirt - to be deterred. Nothing a little gag couldn't fix...

"Oh no, it's nice! I was just surprised. Don't know what I expected, but it wasn't that… ha."

## Mr. BruceBatWayneMan

"I am so sorry, Mr. Wayne-"

"Batman." Bruce – Bat – Mr. Wayne grunts.

"Batman, right." Jerry nods, echoing him. "But you're behind on your last three monthly repayments. We have to seize the Batmobile until further notice, effective immediately."

"But I'm Batman."

"Yeah, I know, Mr. Wayne-"

"Batman."

"-everyone in Gotham City knows, but you're behind on your loan

42

repayments. It's out of my hands. I'm sorry, Mr- Batman." Jerry gestures to no one, to nothing. Shrugs. "Please hand over the keys to your vehicle."

Begrudgingly – he is a man (bat) of the law, Mr. BruceBatWayneMan – he shoves a gloved, spiked, armoured hand into his cloak, into the back pocket of his BatSuit – yes, Robin, it has pockets. It wasn't designed for a woman – and pulls out the keys. He clicks the lock button, causing the headlights to flash. Just proving they're the correct keys. Jerry holds out a hand for the keys.

"Please," Jerry pleads, "don't make this any harder than it has to be. I am on your side, but the law is the law. You signed a contract." Batman throws the keys deeper into the Batcave. Screeching and crying out, a flurry of bats scatter from their hangings in the rocks.

## The Stone

She ain't the one... you always thought she was. You chased and chased. Did what you could to support. Gave a shoulder, to learn on, to cry on. Your heart broke over and over with every tear cried. She broke down and you fell with her, giving all you had in you to pick her back up.

In the end you weren't enough. A mere steppingstone to her realising her greatness again. The stone to sharpen her ruthless blade.

# Streams of Consciousness

## 22/06/2020

Mouth dry. Giggle. Type out- but the fngers, the gfingers don't work, they're so lazy- sloths and their two clawed nails are digging into a tree trunk circling rough brown bark with grooves and rims and sticky out splinters and fingers. Speeding up . is this my normal spped but fingers still lagging and dragging across the board because too lazy to lfit them up akl the way ots not laziness it's a theres no need –

    "is this same girl who has a degree in English?"

Fuck off-

I'm smiling bro I love him and the
fingers are lifting off of the keys, they
are pounding the beat to the doldrum but
the doldrum is keys and the lifts are
strokes and it's like this is a stroke
because one hand is far more active than
the other and I'm watching him play
Minecraft in the top right corner of my
screen and not looking at the keyboard
as I type this out while we're on a date
but it's not a date it's just us hanging out
because we don't always go on dates but
sometimes we just. Hang out. And he's
my boyfriend and my chest is stinging
while typing this and he just said hello as

I typed it and my mouth smiled just a broad, broad grin, and I feel soft and whimsical and if I'm doing this I'm doing it all IN. Damn these eyes are dry.

## 18/01/2020

I fell down off the edge of the castle, where there is a ledge. Hit the ground pretty hard and my phone when flying. Luckily it's fine. RIP to about 6 holes in my tights, one leg - just one - was bleeding fairly bad. Meg wanted food, so we headed over to get her food from Spar. Anyway, I'm not sure how I should write this but I started with how I ended up walking to Spar with bloody legs looking way worse than they are. But also grazing your legs hurts more than you think. Also I should have acted less high around my flatmate. I hope she isn't upset about us smoking and then coming back high. Also I asked Meg to play and God, music sounds better when you're high. Same as food. Made noodles with soy sauce. Spicy food definitely tastes better when you're high. I got a really good grungy picture of cut up tights. Really like it not going to lie.

Cheeks grinning and smiling and "down it" and "you have to" and "don't steal my drink" and "I'm going to shag you."

And the pour and the feeling of floating in and out of the body and who's had to drink there's just me and Erin and someone else who is me and her and the other one and two and nine in the afternoon and floating and I like it and... and truth or dare or ring of fire or he's so aggressive and snobs.

Snobs, a nightclub, a face against the abuser a guy everyone knows a guy with a charming personality a guy with weed in the pocket and a joint on the

picket and a silent on the hand a land a

Mr Wilkes and a down it and a ring of fire

and shit and waterfall because we got a

two and HE SAID SOMEONE'S NAME-

Hozier and Wilkes don't you think

we have a problem?

Cough and coughing up the weed

and sticking in the throat like a piece of

Sellotape with minimal fur just captured

to it a small piece of fluff.

## 13/02/2020

I'm high, I burnt my throat and my
mouth tastes ashy. Not sure how I made
my throat burn. It's rainy. Heavy. It hits
the door. Chloe plays music. Last night
we sat as music rose through the floor.
This ale tastes sweet but it can't take
away the burn. Kind of reminds me of
depression. You can try and drink it away
but that won't work. It's a temporary
relief. Anyway, we had food. Trying to
eat without feeling guilt. Thighs, thick,
oh I got mine for free. Gonna learn to
love my body.

*19/05/2020*

I find that I feel really inspired and creative when I'm stoned, then once I try and create something with that feeling, I just feel horny.

## 21/03/2020

Smoked some bud, nicely toasted I'm watching TV, well, not really watching: my mum owns TV time so I am looking at Eastenders. The adverts so far have been odd, some woman telling me about her trip to Turkey like I even asked, then some diet advert with really oddly drawn women with massive hips. Disturbing. Coronation Street now. I remember that the ginger one had her kids taken off of her for having a working gun. I don't watch Coronation Street and know that somehow? The conversation the current characters have been having was about chocolate. Riveting.

Tricked the cat into thinking my sweets were Dreamies. As soon as she saw it wasn't, she ran away. Why doesn't she love me? Bradley Walsh is so protective over his son, it's adorable.

I just had the realization that Jorge never left San Antonio.

All of the time I spent in Brazil and Paris and Austin and Mexico, Jorge was in San Antonio.

My heart has been broken on three different continents and his has only been broken in one city.

I don't know why it took smoking a joint to realize the enormity of that. The maturity I gained in hyperdrive from packing up my things and unpacking them more times than he has.

**27/01/2020**

I am couch. Melted. Symbiotic. One.

Almost complete.

I spark up for the second time in an hour.

The rumble of the washing machine echoing the thoughts in my mind. I think back to the first time I remembered a washing machine. I was about five. Dead mouse. Crawled in. Chewed a cable. Sparks. I remember my mum hand washing our clothes for weeks after. Still had the machine. Didn't use it. My mum, frustrated and upset. Tired. I understood it to be integral to happiness and success in adulthood.

Adulthood.

Success?

30 children. Responsibility. Professional. Washing machine.

Writing an essay on child human rights. I think, 'what were mine when I was a child?' Why didn't I know I had rights. What are rights? 12 years old. Abused. Parentless. Carer for two younger siblings. Secondary school. Do better. Attain. Balance. Disabled mother. Two siblings. Feed. Shop. Clean. Socialise.

Is it like the birds and the bees? An adult decides when it's appropriate a child should 'know'. Even then, it's a fluffy, scientifically incoherent ramble of stalks, God, wishes; flowers, willies, seeds. Sexually abused children know of sex way before an adult dictates them to be the age appropriate for 'the talk'. After the fact. Told it's natural or dirty. Conflicting. Where is the honesty. It's unsafe.

Dysfunctional family, the child is neglected and abused for years. Knows it doesn't seem right. Compares experience to friends. Doesn't know what this difference means. Told in adulthood means of prevention. After the fact.

Why? At what point between child and

adult is this line drawn? Is it an age? A

calculated intelligence. Responsibility. Is

the line for knowing your human rights

at the same point as the latter?

Why is the mental health of our

children and young adults becoming

increasingly worse? Is it the ease of

knowledge? Internet. Social media. Is it

an increase of awareness? The issues

have always been the same, but we are

more welcoming as a society to talk. Is it

the increasing disparity between

generations? A refusal to adapt and

learn.

I think of Rob Delaney. His skit on not having rights as a kid. Why did it take so long to see change?

## 11/06/2020

I am so happy to be alive in quarantine, without my friends around but they're at the end of my hand and everything isn't as bleak as they make it appear I swear. You have to look for the good it won't just park itself on your doorstep like my dog when he has decided that he's done with our walk so he pulls so hard he yanks the lead out of my hand and I see him waiting when I get home. I find happiness in little things with big impacts. Amazing songs that radiate gratitude. 'Everything is Borrowed' by The Streets does this. So do Disney films, The Incredibles 2 specifically.

Happiness is just an emotion, so when things make you sad you have to find something that makes you happy.

I know that sometimes life is shit, and there's probably going to be times in the future where I feel broken, but what's the use in wallowing in that now when things are so good? I love summer, I'm always so happy in the summer. I think the colour green does wonders for the mind, surrounded by subtly flowing leaves that lean against you gently. A hug from mother nature which lets you know "you're welcome to stay as long as you need." I want more greenery in this area of the garden I'm in. There's a lot, but I want more. I want it to grow over top like a ceiling so it feels like I can hide away for a while. The air brushing on my skin. The clean air that fills my chest. To the colours I see, the birds I hear, the bugs that land on my arm and fight through the long blonde hairs. To the feel of gravel crunching under my foot. To my dog Dave that appears every now and then checking I'm still here. To the two beers and singular joint that gave me this urge to write something, anything.

To the friends that I'm talking to, Paige, sending me her face glowing with happiness. What an amazing feeling to feel when someone you love is happy.

It's a small warmth inside your body that

tells you they're safe, they're okay. If

you're reading this as a writer WRITE

OUTSIDE. My mouth is dry. Very dry. But

the music is still flowing through me.

Okay I'm allowing one emo song.

Skipped it. Think my creative flow dried

up, ain't wrote in like 20 mins and I'm

yawning. Love or freedom. What a

decision. Why do things always end up

being so complicated when they're

actually really simple to start with? I was

just thinking of something so serious in

my head that made a lot of sense of a

serious topic and then I thought I should

write it down and then I forgot what it

was. I am bewildered right now. Frogs.

**23/04/2020**

I wanna put this shit in Comic Sans, it's

such a hated font? I don't understand the

unnecessary hate towards the poor guy.

More love to Comic Sans, people. I got

distracted, sorry. My hands always get

really cold when I smoke lately, it

confuses me. It's also really annoying, I

think that's why I got annoyed by my

hands before because they're just not

working. I keep distracting myself with

music at the moment, it's fucking

awesome how songs sound completely

different when you're sober in

comparison to being high. Like I

discovered a new song today which has

instantly become my new fave and just like many other people, when I find a new fave I will play it to death. Breakkk that replay button. I've had it on so much this evening and it sounded cool, but now it sounds like fucking art. (The song is UK Apache with Shy FX – 'Original Nuttah 25', give it a listen). Another artists that's like that is Soom T, her voice is like reggae butter.

Ain't it crazy how we are all currently living through something that will be in GCSE history exams one day, Rona just screwing up the whole planet the dickhead. Food time, hold on. Okay so seriously what is the deal with mental illness right. Like after I have smoked and that heaviness that you normally carry around just disappears, like is that how normal people feel? Weightless? I wonder if that feeling is something specific. I mean I have bipolar so I obviously my "heavy" levels come and go in extremities. I wonder what it would be like to be a normal functioning human with fully working organs too, stupid diabetes, why was a diabetic born with a sweet tooth? Where is the fairness in the universe for that shit. I swear when I die I'll have some stern words with some people upstairs, I'll be storming up those stairs to heaven ready to slap a bitch. I took a big ol' food break, now watching

that Sing movie 'cause I fancied

watching some animated animals

singing. It's a shame Taron Egerton is

such a prick in real life.

# 21/03/2020

Well say you're Jon Johnson or whoever,

and you enjoy physics and guitar and

Italian food and so on but behind all of

that, you're also an eddy in the

undulating energy of the world, all the

vibrational frequencies at all levels from

atomic to audial, visual to even your

sleep cycles, heartbeat, breathing and so

on, harmonise together to make you, Jon

Johnson, pop into existence and grow

until eventually they unravel and move

on to become other things.

## 15/03/2020

The universe in any instant is like a
pattern of ripples on the surface of a
multidimensional ocean. An ocean can
never have the same pattern of ripples
across it and so in the same way the
universe can never be the same as a
previous instant, and the harder you try
to cling to a past image of the universe
the more stressed out you'll get when it
won't return to that state.

So I guess in this way it's not like
an intellect but like how waves
superimpose on each other, and create
their own larger waves, which in turn

make swells, I think it's like that but with varying forms of vague energy.

Or perhaps how sometimes in rivers, little eddies form and linger, life might just be the so called "eddies" which can, (if conditions are right) spawn their own eddies to carry on their energy.

## 09/05/2020

Trying to smoke so damn quickly because I missed my window of opportunity hopefully it'll encourage me to think quicker too. I feel like after three years of sneaking around my grandparents to smoke up I've definitely learned some of the patterns and triggers of when to smoke. It's always frustrating when they break the routine though. And then my mind goes blank. To be fair I'm trying to listen for footsteps coming around the corner because I'm trying to be at least slightly sly. Slightly sly to get high is definitely gonna be the name of my stoner album.

If I ever manage to do the music thing.

God damn my lungs hurt. Asthma gets in

the way of my smoking habits. Door shut

gotta clip in the J and sneak away. Now I

get a J and a half in the next window.

Just watched the toilet roll flip and land I

don't know why I'm finding it so funny

but my cheeks won't stop grinning and

Lord Huron is playing and this was meant

to be a short story about Phil about

magic about unicorns about making them

cry, making them sad and harvesting

their tears for healing and- my left hand

is strained. The joint muscles pull.

A slight tremble.

A shaking of my external limbs,

punching of the keyboard keys clack

clack clack and a sip of coke zero to

soothe this drying throat. Never mind

Coke zero tastes fucking weird. Gonna drink it anyway. One might call that a mistake. I might be the aforementioned one.

# Where to Seek Help

If you are concerned about the use, or misuse, of drugs – whether for yourself, or for someone you know, please seek professional or medical advice. Your GP is a good and confidential place to start, and below are some free and confidential resources that can help you start your journey. This information is correct as of August 2020.

## England

### Mind

www.mind.org.uk

0300 123 3393

info@mind.org.uk

### FRANK

www.talktofrank.com

0300 1236600

frank@talktofrank.com

## Northern Ireland

Addiction NI

www.addictionni.com

028 9066 44 34

enquiries@addictionni.com

Cassiobury Court

www.cassioburycourt.com

0800 001 4070

info@cassioburycourt.com

# Éire

## DRUGS.ie

www.drugs.ie

1800 459 459

helpline@hse.ie

## Addiction Recovery

www.addictionrecoveryireland.ie

087 655 1565

## Scotland

### Scottish Drugs Services Directory

www.scottishdrugservices.com

0141 221 1175

enquiries@sdf.org.uk

### Port of Call

www.portofcall.com

0808 301 8727

## Wales

### DAN 24/7

www.dan247.org.uk

0808 808 2234

Text DAN to 81066

### Recovery Cymru

www.recoverycymru.org.uk

01446 734220

info@recoverycymru.org.uk

# Further Reading

If the contents of this book has inspired you to learn more about cannabis use and its link to the creative arts, the selected bibliography below contains an array of literature all about the subject.

Jones, Nick. 2013. *Spliffs: A Celebration of Cannabis Culture*.

Lee, Martin A. 2012. *Smoke Signals: A Social History of Marijuana – Medical, Recreational, and Scientific*.

Hill, Kevin P. 2015. *Marijuana: The Unbiased Truth about the World's Most Popular Weed.*

Hecht, Peter. 2014. *Weed Land: Inside America's Marijuana Epicenter and How Pot Went Legit.*

Baudelaire, Charles. 1860. *The Artificial Paradises.*

Herer, Jack. 1985. *The Emperor Wears No Clothes.*

Cortes, Ricardo. 2005. *It's Just a Plant: a children's story about marijuana.*

Plant, Sadie. 1999. *Writing on Drugs.*

Printed in Poland
by Amazon Fulfillment
Poland Sp. z o.o., Wrocław

62139747R00052